ZONDERKIDZ

Always Daddy's Princess
Copyright © 2013 by Karen Kingsbury
Illustrations © 2013 by Valeria Docampo

Requests for information should be addressed to:

Zonderkidz, Grand Rapids, Michigan 49530

Library of Congress Cataloging-in-Publication Data
Kingsbury, Karen.
    Always Daddy's princess / by Karen Kingsbury.
        p. cm.
        Summary: Simple, rhyming text celebrates a father's pride and joy, from his daughter's
birth to his granddaughter's, interspersed with relevant Bible passages.
        ISBN 978-0-310-71647-1 (hardcover)
        [1. Stories in rhyme. 2. Fathers and daughters—Fiction 3. Christian life—Fiction.]
I. Title.
PZ8.3.K6145Alw 2013
[E]—dc23   2011034996

Published in association with the literary agency of Alive Communications, Inc.,
7680 Goddard Street, Suite 200, Colorado Springs, CO 80920.
www.alivecommunications.com

Zonderkidz is a trademark of Zondervan.

Editor: Barbara Herndon
Art direction & design: Jody Langley

Printed in China

12 13 14 15 16 17 /LPC/ 6 5 4 3 2 1

To Donald, my very own prince charming
Kelsey, my bright sunshine
Tyler, my favorite song
Sean, my smiley boy
Josh, my gentle giant
EJ, my chosen one
Austin, my miracle child
And to God Almighty, who has—for now—blessed me with these.
—K.K.

For you, daddy, who has always been on my side.
—V.D.

Always Daddy's PRINCESS

KAREN KINGSBURY

ILLUSTRATED BY VALERIA DOCAMPO

ZONDERkidz

ZONDERVAN.com/
AUTHORTRACKER
follow your favorite authors

It's a Girl!

Blow the trumpet, sound the horn,
daddy's princess has been born!

"It is a day for you to sound the trumpets." — NUMBERS 29:1

"Every good and perfect gift is from above." — JAMES 1:17

Eyes so bright and laughter fair,
he buys a pink bow for her hair.
He loves her more than words can say,
his princess, born this happy day.

"He will yet fill your mouth with laughter and your lips with shouts of joy." — JOB 8:21

And when the little girl turns five
her dad stays close, right by her side.
A crown upon her pretty head,
she listens to the things he says.
Well-mannered at the Royal Tea,
his sweet princess, all grins and glee.

The girl turns double digits—ten!
Pink soccer cleats and practice then
dad cheers her on and shouts her name
from sidelines at a thousand games.
Come rain or shine he sees her play,
his princess, star of every day.

"God is within her, she will not fall; God will help her at break of day." — PSALM 46:5

"Clothe yourself with splendor and majesty." — PSALM 45:3

Middle school, she's thirteen now,
friends and clothes and dad learns how
to sit through all her fashion shows
with crazy jeans and painted toes,
all giggles, braces, "Daddy, please!"
His princess girl with knobby knees.

His girl grows taller,
sweet sixteen ...
Boys and music,
fine cuisine.

She shows her dad
her driving skill,

But needs a little practice still!

At prom a beauty in her dress,
his little girl, his sweet princess.

College takes her far from home.
Then, travel: London, Paris, Rome ...

But even when she's far away,
his heart is hers and so he prays,
for his girl's life has just begun,
his princess, now at twenty-one.

"You know when I sit and when I rise; you perceive my thoughts from afar." — PSALM 139:2

A pretty ring, her wedding day,
her dad knows his girl cannot stay.
He walks her proudly down the aisle
then steps aside, a wink, a smile.

He gives a toast—lifelong romance!
Then asks his princess for a dance.

"Therefore what God has joined together, let no one separate."— MARK 10:9

"A time to dance." — ECCLESIASTES 3:4

Blow the trumpet, sound the horn,
grandpa's princess has been born!

"My heart rejoices in the LORD; in the LORD my horn is lifted high." — 1 SAMUEL 2:1

Eyes so bright and laughter fair.
He buys a pink bow for her hair.
His heart, all joy and happiness,
TWO princess girls, a life so blessed.